hammering

pretending

dribbling

swinging

chatting

blowing

building

resting

catching

For Brenda

First U.S. edition 1994
Published in Great Britain in 1994 by Walker Books Ltd., London.

Library of Congress Cataloging-in-Publication Data

Hughes, Shirley.
Chatting / Shirley Hughes.—1st U.S. ed.
Summary: A little girl describes many different kinds of chatting,
including chats with the cat, with friends, in the park, and at the supermarket.
ISBN 1-56402-340-0
[1. Conversation—Fiction.] I. Title.
PZ7.H87395Cgf 1994
[E]—dc20 93-22747

2 4 6 8 10 9 7 5 3 1

Printed in Italy

The pictures in this book were done in colored pencils,
watercolor, and pen line.

Candlewick Press
2067 Massachusetts Avenue
Cambridge, Massachusetts 02140

Chatting

Shirley Hughes

CANDLEWICK PRESS
CAMBRIDGE, MASSACHUSETTS

I like chatting.

I chat to the cat,

and I chat in the car.

I chat with friends in the park,

and with the lady at the supermarket.

7
8
9
10

Grown-ups like chatting too.

Sometimes these chats go on
for a very long time.

The lady next door is
an especially good chatter.

When Mom is busy she says that there are just too many chatterboxes around.

So I go off and chat to Bemily—
but she never says a word.

The baby likes
a chat on his
toy telephone.

He makes
a lot of calls.

But I can chat
with Grandma
and Grandpa
on the real
telephone.

Some of the best chats
of all are with Dad,

when he comes to
say good night.

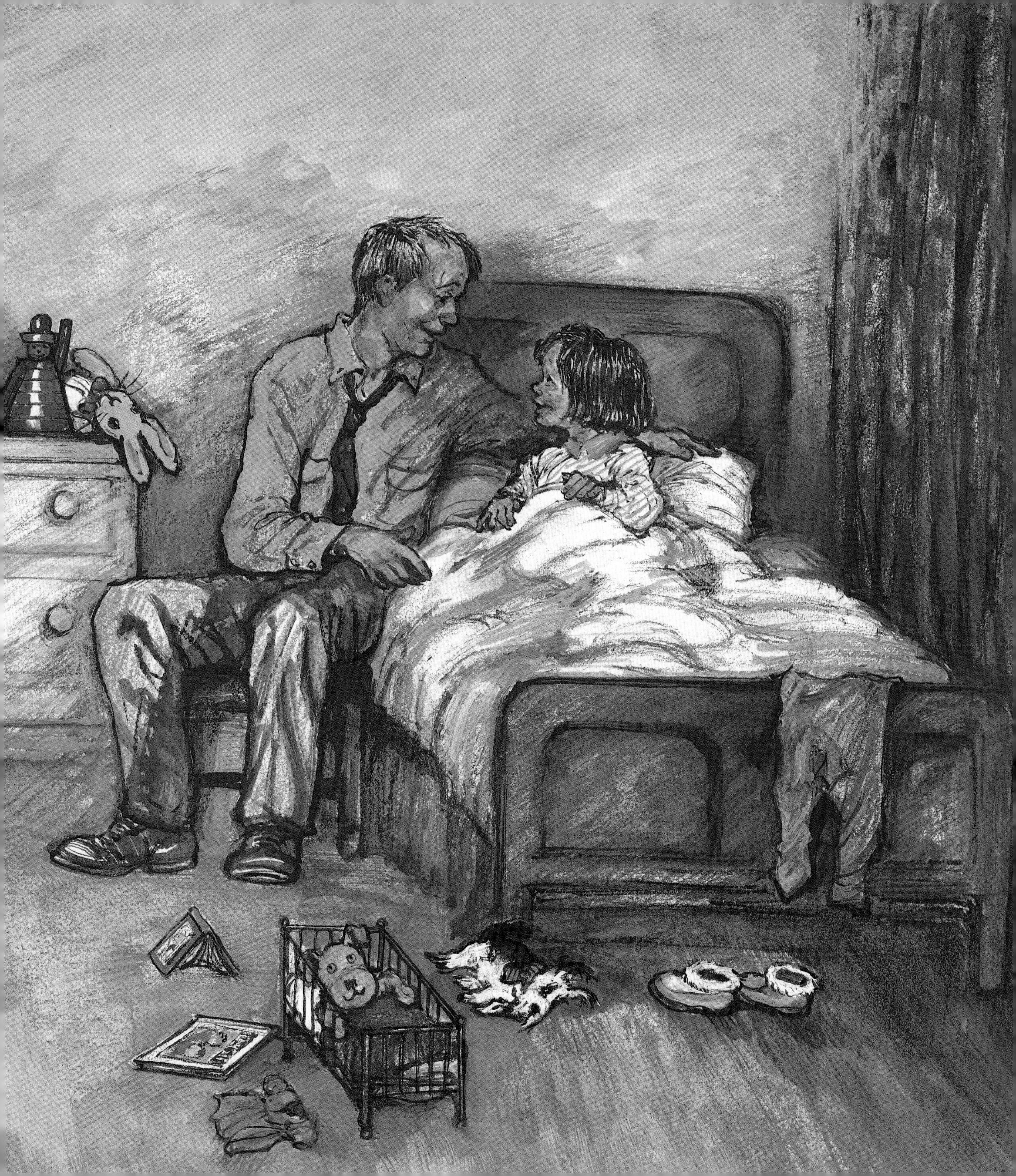

laughing

aching

pushing

pouring

chatting

hopping

sulking

kissing

sneezing